MY
DOG
MOUSE

Eva Lindström

GECKO PRESS

This edition first published in 2017 by Gecko Press
PO Box 9335, Marion Square, Wellington 6141, New Zealand
info@geckopress.com

Text and illustrations © Eva Lindström 2016
English language edition © Gecko Press Ltd 2017

Original title: *Musse* © Lilla Piratförlaget AB 2016

Distributed in the United States and Canada by Lerner Publishing Group, www.lernerbooks.com
Distributed in the United Kingdom by Bounce Sales and Marketing, www.bouncemarketing.co.uk
Distributed in Australia by Scholastic Australia, www.scholastic.com.au
Distributed in New Zealand by Upstart Distribution, www.upstartpress.co.nz

The cost of this translation was defrayed by a subsidy from
the Swedish Arts Council, gratefully acknowledged.

Translated by Julia Marshall
Edited by Penelope Todd
Typesetting by Katrina Duncan
Printed in China by Everbest Printing Co Ltd,
an accredited ISO 14001 & FSC certified printer

ISBN hardback: 978-1-776571-48-2
ISBN paperback: 978-1-776571-49-9

For more curiously good books, visit www.geckopress.com

I love Mouse.

"Can I take Mouse for a walk?" I ask, and I'm always allowed.

We set off, very slowly. Mouse walks at a snail's pace.
He stops at lampposts and fences and sniffs for a long
time. Sometimes he looks up at me and then I usually say
something. I maybe say something like "old man" in a very
nice voice, not my usual one.

He's old and fat with ears as thin as
pancakes. His walk is a kind of waddle
and he's always pleased to see me.

When he opens his mouth you can see all his teeth. He's too kind to bite and I'm kind back, then he licks me, so I pat him again, and then he yawns and I have time to count his teeth before he closes his mouth.

At the park, I take off his collar. We sit there on the grass and eat our picnic. It's the usual, and Mouse helps himself to mine, too, while I look carefully at a particular cloud.

We walk as slowly as we can.
All the others go past us. We are always the
slowest. We take a small step and then we pause,
then another step and pause, and so we go.
Step, pause. Step, pause. Step, pause.

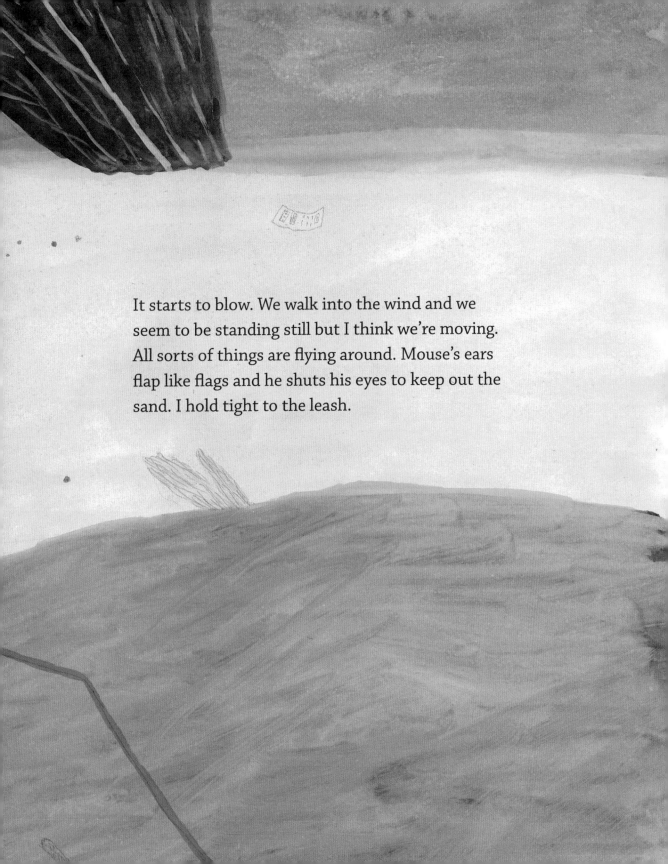

It starts to blow. We walk into the wind and we
seem to be standing still but I think we're moving.
All sorts of things are flying around. Mouse's ears
flap like flags and he shuts his eyes to keep out the
sand. I hold tight to the leash.

It has stopped blowing now and Mouse's ears hang straight down again.

I have two meatballs in my pocket for us to eat. I hold them out and he takes them both in one bite.

Then we keep going, at our usual pace.
When we turn off to the right we see the
house where Mouse lives.

Did it go well? That's what Mouse's owner
asks. I say that it went very, very well.
   She says thank you and takes the leash
and Mouse follows her inside. I stand there
till I can't see him any more.

I wish Mouse was mine.